lauren child

S0-AQK-456

I am
TOO
absolutely
small for
school

SCHOLASTIC INC.
New York Toronto London Auckland Sydney
Mexico City New Delhi Hong Kong Buenos Aires

for Sofie and her
invisible friend
Søren Lorensen

and for Maisie, Clemmie,
Molly and Ella

ISBN-13: 978-0-439-87580-6

ISBN-10: 0-439-87580-3

Copyright © 2003 by Lauren Child. All rights reserved. Published by Scholastic Inc., 557 Broadway, New York, NY 10012, by arrangement with Candlewick Press. SCHOLASTIC and associated logos are trademarks and/or registered trademarks of Scholastic Inc.

12 11 10 9 8 7 6 5 4 3 2 1   7 8 9 10 11 12/0

Printed in the U.S.A.   40

First Scholastic paperback printing, November 2007

Absolutely thank you to Goldy for taking all the photographs so beautifully.

Thank you to Simon for his utterly invaluable comments.

This book was typeset in Officina Serif Book and Badloc.

The illustrations were done in mixed media.

huge

giantish

big

biggish

smallish

Slightly small

small

tiny

teeny

eeny weeny

Lola

says,

"I am **absolutely** not **BIG**.

I am still

really quite small."

She says, "I probably do not have **time** to go to **school.** I am too **extremely busy** doing i**mport**a**nt** t**h**i**n**g**s** at **home."**

I say,
"At school
you will learn
numbers and how to
count up to one hundred."

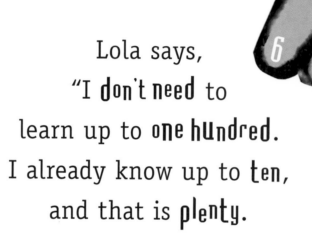

Lola says,
"I don't need to
learn up to one hundred.
I already know up to ten,
and that is plenty.

I have ten fingers. And
also I have ten toes.

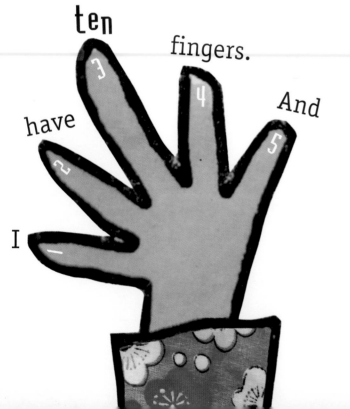

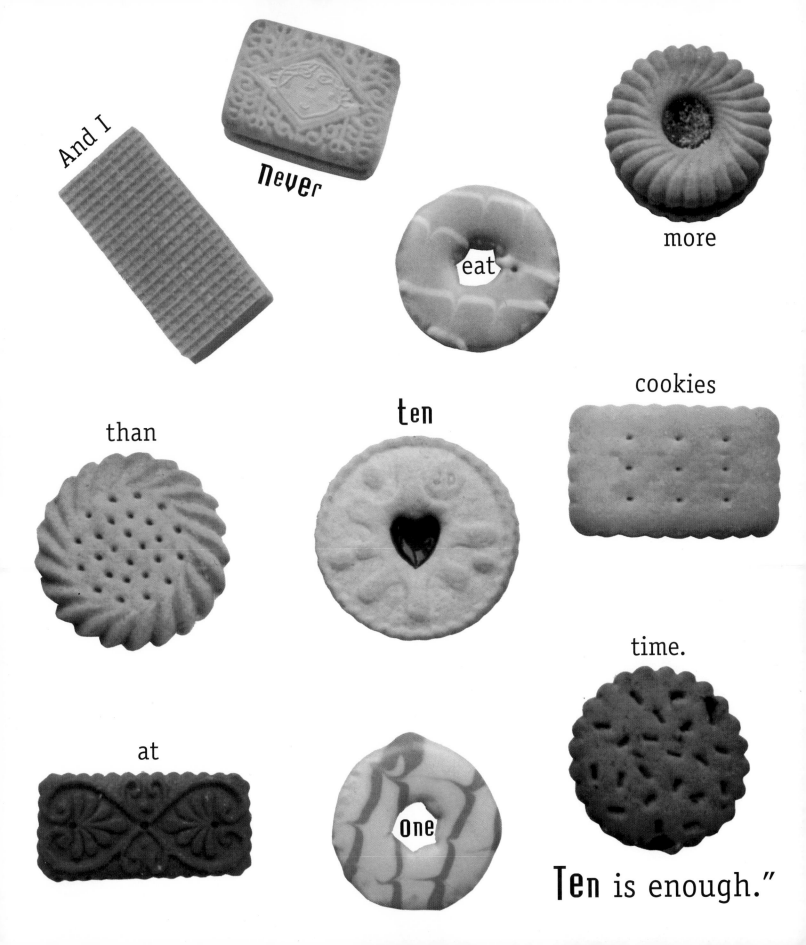

And I

never

more

eat

than

ten

cookies

time.

at

One

Ten is enough."

"But Lola," I say, "what if eleven eager elephants all wanted a treat.

I say,
"And what about learning your **letters**, Lola?
If you know how to write,
you can send cards to
people you like."

"Lola says, "I like to talk on the telephone.

It's more friendly and straightaway."

"But not everyone has a telephone, you know, Lola," I say.

"Who doesn't?" says Lola.

"Santa Claus," I say. "You have to write him a special note and send it to the North Pole to tell the

elves your Christmas wish. Otherwise the elves might get your wish mixed up."

"I didn't know that, Charlie," says Lola.

"And Lola," I say,
"don't you want to
read words? Then you will
be able to **read** your
own **books.** And understand
secret messages written
on the fridge."

Lola says,
"I know lots of **secrets.**
I don't need to **read words,**
and I've got all my
books in my head.
If I can't remember, I
can just make them up."

there is
pink milk
in this
fridge

"But Lola," I say, "what would you do if there was an ever-so-angry ogre who would not go to sleep unless you read him his favorite bedtime story?"

"I don't know, Charlie,"

says Lola.

Then Lola says,
        "I would like to
read to an ogre and
        count up elephants and
send notes to the North Pole.
But I absolutely will NOT
        ever wear a schooliform.
I do not like wearing the
same as other people."

I say,
        "But Lola, you
won't have to wear a
        school uniform. At our
school you can wear
        whatever you like."

"Oh," says Lola.
        "You wait there. I know
exactly what I can wear. . . ."

"Well, Lola," I say,
    "that's certainly stylish,

        but you **cannot** go to school
dressed as a **crocodile**."

Lola says,
    "This is **not** a **crocodile**. This is **a alligator**."

I say, "You can't really go
        as **an** alligator, either."

"Why
not?"
says
Lola.

"I like to wear stripes," says Lola, "but what will I do at lunchtime? You know I will **neve**r NOT EVER eat a **school lunch**."

My sister, Lola, is fussy about food.

I say,

"But Lola, you can take your very own **packed lunch** in your very own lunch box."

Lola says, "I do not want to eat at school, **alone**, all by myself, on my own."

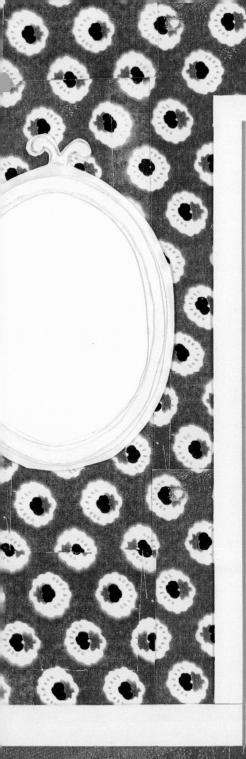

I say, "But Lola, at school you will meet lots of new **friends**. You can have **lunch** with one of them."

Then Lola says, "But I already have **my friend**, Soren Lorensen. I like to have **lunch** at **home** with him."

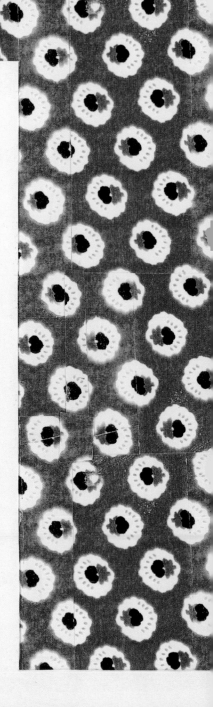

Soren Lorensen is Lola's invisible friend. No one knows what he looks like.

Walking to school, Lola is all wobbly.

She says, "Soren Lorensen is feeling slightly not very well.

He is worried he will not be able to count numbers, do letters, and read words, and no one will

"Lola," I say, "it will be **okay.**

You'll be fi**ne.**

I bet

you'll

both

have

a

really

good

time.

And

after

school

we'll have pink milk at home."

talk to him, so he will be all by himself, on his own."

But all day I am worried.

I don't see Lola at recess,

and she's nowhere at lunch.

When school gets out, she's not by her peg.

But then

there

she

is,

and she's

not all alone,

by herself.

She's

hopping

along

home

with

somebody

else. . . .

At home, I say,
    "Lola, I **told you** that you would
            have a **good time**."
And Lola says,
    "Oh I know, Charlie, I was not
worried. It was Soren Lorensen
            who was nervous, **not me**.
    I was **fine**."